Arthur Throws a Tantrum

Illustrations Anne Villeneuve

Translation by Sarah Cummins

Formac Publishing Company Limited
Halifax, Nova Scotia 1993

Originally published as Les barricades d'Arthur

Copyright © by les éditions de la courte échelle inc.

Translation copyright © 1993 by Formac Publishing Company Limited.

Canadian Cataloguing in Publication Data

Gauthier, Gilles, 1943-

  [Barricades d'Arthur. English]

  Arthur Throws a Tantrum

  (First novel series)
  .
  Translation of: Les barricades d'Arthur.
  ISBN 0-88780-221-4 (pbk.).   ISBN 0-88780-222-2 (bound)

I. Villeneuve, Anne. II. Title. III. Title: Barricades d'Arthur. English. IV. Series.

PS8551.N42B3713   1992   jC843'.54   C92-098706-0
PZ7.A53Ar 1992

Formac Publishing Company Limited
5502 Atlantic Street
Halifax, N.S. B3H 1G4

Printed and bound in Canada.

Table of Contents

To Zoe Egenna ... who has given me
dozens of good ideas.

1
Just like Annie McCubbin's

One Sunday morning Arthur Goodberry threw the biggest tantrum of his life. It lasted three minutes and fifteen seconds, and Arthur managed to destroy almost everything.

Afterwards, with his head under his pillow, Arthur lay lamenting. He wept and felt so ashamed that he wished he could just disappear. Either disappear completely or become the tiniest thing in town.

He wished he could become tinier than a flea. Tinier than a

flea's knee! Tinier than the flea on the knee of a flea!

Arthur felt so ashamed that he didn't dare lift his head. He went back over everything he'd done.

First he remembered chewing the nicest picture of his dad and then tearing it into tiny pieces — *SLASH!*

Then he went to his toy chest and stomped on his entire mask collection, trampled his chemistry set, and scattered hundreds of creepy crawlies all around the room.

Then he ripped up his new T-shirt, twisted his eight new water pistols out of shape, and flung a glass of pineapple juice against the ceiling — *SPLASH!*

He remembered, but he

wished he could forget the terrible thing he had done to the smallest of his twelve stuffed basset hounds.

The very second he opened his eyes, Arthur saw it lying at the foot of his bed. Its tail and ears were torn off and its eyes were dangling by a thread. His favourite basset hound. Arthur swallowed hard.

Clenching his fists, he leaped out of bed, sprang to the door, and locked it. Then he pushed his biggest dresser against the door and piled everything he could find on top of it, all the way up to the ceiling.

Then he yelled with all his might, "Either I get a REAL basset hound, just like Annie McCubbin's, or I will NEVER

EVER come out of my room again!"

2
Standing guard

Arthur leaned against the pile of furniture and toys and caught his breath. Over the beating of his heart he listened for a word, a sound, a sign from his father.

Maybe his father was playing dead. The hall was as still and silent as Dracula's tomb.

Puzzled, Arthur scratched his noggin. Then he seriously wondered whether his father had not gone deaf as a doorknob. After all, he was already bald as a doorknob!

Thinking it over, Arthur concluded that his father was

plotting something. Some kind of dirty trick. So he screamed loud enough to drown out the sirens on sixty fire trucks, "William Goodberry, I'm warning you! To break down my barricades, you're going to need a bulldozer! Or else a tank!"

Dizzy from all that screaming, Arthur smiled. He knew his dad had no bulldozer and no tank. All he had was a minuscule snowblower and a pitiful little lawnmower!

And he could not break down anything with the stuff in the tricks and the jokes store that he owns.

Arthur imagined his father vanquished, in tears and down on his knees, begging forgiveness.

"Arthur, I was wrong. I'm

sorry, Arthur. Open the door for your daddy, please."

Arthur could not hold back his snickers. He knew just what he would do.

He would play dead. That would show his dad!

After a while, since not a creature was stirring in the house, Arthur decided to stand guard in front of his barricade.

He sat there, confidently twiddling his thumbs. He had forgotten that the window of his room was WIDE OPEN. He didn't know that someone was sneaking up to it on tiptoe.

3
No collar and no tags

The first thing Arthur heard was an earsplitting *BANG!* Then a voice yelling, "Arthur Goodberry, are you crazy or what?"

Arthur froze in fright. He felt as if his heart had leapt up to the ceiling — *BADONG!*

Weak and floppy as a rag doll, Arthur turned around. How foolish he felt at seeing Annie McCubbin, his best friend.

In relief, he made a face and went over to the window. He begged Annie to keep her voice down and to keep out, because he had barricaded himself in.

Curious as a cat, Annie stuck her nose in the window anyway. She looked all around the room, and her eyes grew as big and round as doughnut holes. Clutching her head in both hands, she said, "Yi-yi-yi-yi-yi-yi-YI!"

A bit embarrassed, Arthur whispered, "Things are a bit untidy in here. It's all because of my dad."

Annie was impressed. "A bit untidy! You can say that again! I've never seen anything like it in my life."

She craned her neck to get a better look. The ENORMITY of the catastrophe made her think that Arthur's dad must have told him he couldn't have any more bananas, or stink bombs, or itching powder.

Finally Arthur had to admit that he had flipped out because his dad wouldn't believe him.

"Wouldn't believe what?" inquired Annie.

"Well," said Arthur, "he wouldn't believe that I had found a real basset hound, with NO collar and NO tags, exactly like your basset hound Quincy!"

Annie was surprised. She nodded, paused, waved her hands in the air, burst out laughing, and then declared, "Arthur Goodberry, if you mean you found a short-legged, long-bodied, purebred basset hound like MY Quincy, then I don't believe you either!"

To make her message clear, she added, "I am quite certain that I am the owner of the sole, unique, one and only basset hound in all of Hinksville."

Arthur, who had been as white as chalk, now turned as green as spinach. Watch out, Annie McCubbin! Arthur does not like his word to be doubted, especially not today!

Swift as a swallow, he knocked Annie overboard *VLANG!* She fell headfirst into a dandelion patch — *POOF!*

4
Bar the window,
bar the door!

Fifteen seconds later, Annie's head reappeared at the window sill. As if nothing had happened, she said, "Are you crazy or what? Are you out of your mind? Have you forgotten that I am ambidextrous?"

She stuck her nose back in the room. "I've got two things to say. And woe betide you, Arthur Goodberry, if you shut that window in my face!"

As a matter of fact, Arthur had just been about to slam the window—*SHLACK*—in front of her nose, but he held back. He was very cautious around ambidextrous people.

He knew that Annie McCubbin was possessed of many special powers. He had seen how she had scared Charlotte Peever from ever visiting his dad again. He knew she could do anything, with either her left hand or her right hand. That's what ambidextrous means.

And since Arthur did not wish to be changed into a toad or a dinosaur or a tow truck, he refrained from slamming down the window.

Cautiously and quietly, Arthur muttered, "I give you two minutes to say what you have to say. Then ..."

"Then what?" demanded Annie,

sneering.

"Then nothing," Arthur answered sheepishly.

Glowing with triumph, Annie casually asked, "I only wondered WHERE exactly you found this piddly little basset hound of yours?"

Arthur wished he could flatten her underfoot like a pancake. But to get rid of her sooner, he answered, "In the elevator in Charlotte Peever's building. I had gone there to tell her to stop gossiping about my father's store. And I found the little puppy. All alone, sad as can be, abandoned! And with NO collar and NO tags! So there!"

Unfortunately for Arthur, Ambidextrous Annie had no intention of leaving until she had found out all there was to know. She rested her chin on the window ledge and, half-curious, half-mocking, asked, "Then what?"

So Arthur had to tell her how the little baby basset hound had followed him home, and how he had fed it on chicken breast, cookies, jujubes, and milk. And how the puppy had peed all over the rug and how Arthur had cleaned it up and put the puppy down for a nap on his bed.

Arthur had wanted to give the puppy a name. He couldn't decide between Aldo, after Al Doloroso, who worked in his father's store, and Banana, after his favourite fruit.

So finally he hadn't named the puppy at all. His father came

home. And his father had told him the dog most certainly did belong to someone and made him take it back to exactly the same place where he had found it.

Telling his story made Arthur feel bad all over again. The more he thought about his father and about the little basset hound, the more he felt like crying.

Arthur sniffled and blew his nose — *PTCHOO!* Then, caring

not a fig newton for Arthur's sorrow, Annie said, "In any case, MY Quincy came straight from Texas, in an airplane. He's not a poor abandoned stray, like your ALDO or BANANA!"

And before she finally made herself scarce, Annie added, "Just let me give you a word of warning, about your father. I would not need an atomic bomb to break through your barricades. I would just throw a little stink bomb through your bedroom window. And I think your father knows where to find a stink bomb!"

This kindly advice made Arthur feel like a turkey. Like a goose. Like a booby. Like a dodo bird.

When his supposedly best friend had left, Arthur rushed to

the window, shut it, locked it, and sealed the cracks with tape.

Then, to be on the safe side, he covered all the glass with paint and ink. He piled six big shelves from his bookcase in front of it and pulled the curtains shut—*SWISH*—as far as they would go.

By then, it was so dark in his room that Arthur had to light his frog lamp and his bedside bat lamp.

Arthur settled cosily down between his two barricades and murmured to himself with satisfaction, "Let him come, with all the stink bombs he wants. He'll never get one past the door OR the window. No way!"

5
Four peanuts

Arthur spent almost an hour dreaming up a thousand plans to thwart any dastardly scheme his father might devise.

For an hour he lay with his ear to the carpet, waiting to detect the merest movement, the slightest sound, a breath, a murmur, a tiny *SWISH SWISH* somewhere behind him, beside him, in the hall or under his bed.

Poor Arthur didn't feel like playing, or sewing the ears of his stuffed animal back on, or exercising his left hand so that he could be ambidextrous.

Time passed so slowly that each minute seemed like a weekend. Arthur finally decided that this had to be the most boring Sunday of his entire life!

He glanced at his watch. It was two o'clock.

Arthur became aware that the bowl of cereal he had gulped down early that morning had now reached the soles of his feet.

Automatically he reached into his pocket for the package of gum he always kept there. He opened it, shook it once, twice. NOTHING! The box was empty. Absolutely empty!

In desperation Arthur ran to the closet and looked through all the pockets of his pants, his windbreaker, his T-shirts, jeans, and raincoat. Still nothing!

He pulled open his drawers and dumped out everything that hadn't already been dumped out. He crawled under his bed. Rummaged through his wastepaper basket. And finally he found an old bag of peanuts with four peanuts inside.

Carefully Arthur laid his precious treasure on the bed. With sinking heart he drew out the peanuts, one by one, and placed them in a row on his pillow.

His mouth watering, he gazed at the trickles of pineapple juice dribbling from the ceiling. Arthur was famished. He ate the first peanut, then the second, then the third.

Arthur decided to save the

fourth peanut for supper. But his stomach emitted such a terrifying rumble that he took the peanut and just placed it on his tongue, to suck it. Then he decided to chew it as slowly as possible.

He chewed and chewed, thinking of the half-dozen doughnuts languishing on the top shelf of the refrigerator. And the butter-scotch pie tucked in on the bottom shelf. And the macaroni and cheese that his father always made for Sunday lunch.

Then Arthur thought about bananas. And the more he thought about bananas, the hungrier he got. And the hungrier he got, the more he thought it was unfair. His father was a monster! The worst monster in the whole world.

Finally, as the last of the last peanut was swallowed, he heard a strange reaction from his stomach. It sounded like ten cats in a growling contest.

All at once, something horrifying began to dawn on Arthur. Now

he understood why there was no move or sound from his father. Arthur realized that his father had decided to let him STARVE TO DEATH.

Defiantly Arthur yelled at the top of his lungs: "William Goodberry, I don't care if you don't let me have any chocolate doughnuts or butterscotch pie! I don't care, because the whole world will know that you let your only child die of hunger!" Then Arthur burst into tears. He was still sniffling when he heard a kind of *SWISH SWISH*, like something scuffling just outside his door.

He stopped sniffling. He held his breath. With his whole body tensed, he listened with all his might.

After three minutes, he had to give up. It was only gnawing hunger that was driving him crazy and making him hear things!

6
A super genius plan

At forty-eight minutes past two, Arthur was still barricaded in his room, and he was fast asleep.

Arthur had thought long and hard and had managed to come up with a solution to two of his three problems.

Just before falling asleep he had devised a super genius plan for dealing with "F" and "A".

It was simple. In order to get food, he would wait until night time. At the first snores of "F" ("F" stood for Father), he would dismantle "B". ("B" was the barricade in front of his door.) The other barricade was "W" (for window, of course).

So, at the first snores of "F", Arthur would dismantle "B". Then he would slip silently into the kitchen. He would remove everything he could eat or drink from "F"'s refrigerator. Then he would return to his room. He would quickly rebuild "B" and check "W" just in case. And then he would eat as much as he liked.

Afterwards he could fall asleep with nary a care, because he could repeat the identical tactical move the next night, and the next, and so on until the end of time.

The plan for "A" was even simpler. ("A", of course, was

Annie McCubbin.) In short, Arthur had decided never to see her again! Not her and not "Q" either. ("Q" was her piddly little dog Quincy.)

So if "A" should come tapping at "W" with her piddly little "Q", Arthur would just play dead, exactly like "F" had been doing all day long.

"A" would get discouraged and would give up any idea of coming back and tapping at "W" to bug him with her piddly little "Q".

Unfortunately, Arthur had not yet found a solution to problem number three.

It would be very difficult to find another little stray dog somewhere. Another little basset puppy just as sweet and nice and sad as the one his father had made him take back.

So, while trying to dream up a way of getting another little basset hound for his very own, Arthur finally fell asleep.

And as he slumbered on, Mr. Goodberry returned home from a long trip in his car.

The poor man was totally in the dark! He knew nothing about the tantrum, the barricades, or the super genius plan.

He knew nothing because, as soon as Arthur had left to return the puppy to Charlotte Peever's building, he had jumped into his car and driven away.

He had seen how unhappy Arthur was and wanted to cheer him up with a big surprise.

Mr. Goodberry had searched far and wide around town. Finally, he had to go to a kennel on the outskirts of the big city before he found the darlingest little basset hound imaginable.

Now, returning home,

Mr. Goodberry felt a little disappointed. The house seemed so empty, so quiet! He figured Arthur had gone to play some-

where. At Annie McCubbin's house, maybe, or with another friend.

Since he was feeling as hungry as a horse, Mr. Goodberry popped the huge dish of macaroni and cheese he had prepared last night into the oven.

Waiting for Arthur to come back, he whistled. He whistled loud and shrill and ceaselessly, as was his wont when he was feeling impatient and extremely happy.

7
I love my dad best of all!

The delicious smell of macaroni and cheese wafted through the house. The surprise for Arthur was exploring the hall from one end to the other. Arthur snoozed on.

As he slept, he dreamed of bananas. Piles of bananas. Not surprising, for in his dream, Arthur was in the depths of the jungle with a dozen orangutans!

What was strange was the way the bananas tasted. They tasted like … macaroni and cheese!

And, stranger yet, a banana peel fell to the ground and began to bark — *WOOF WOOF* — like a puppy!

In his dream, Arthur heard a scratching sound. Then he clearly saw a little basset hound crawl out of the banana peel. The little dog was whimpering.

Still dreaming, Arthur wondered if the dog was crying because it was lost in Africa. Or maybe it was afraid of the orangutans.

Arthur picked the puppy up and held it in his arms. He rocked it and crooned to it and comforted it. Behind him, Arthur could hear whistling. The whistling was coming closer. It became so real that Arthur woke up!

Although his eyes were wide open, Arthur thought he must still be dreaming. But he could still hear a scratching noise at

his own door! He could still smell macaroni and cheese in his own room! And he could hear somebody whistling in his own house!

Arthur realized that he was no longer in Africa. It was still Sunday, and it was his father whistling as he made lunch. And there was something alive outside his door, scratching to be let in!

Arthur cast a dismayed look around. The disaster, the catastrophe, the mess were so terrible! Horrified, Arthur thought of his father.

And the more he thought of his father, the more he recalled the worst tantrum of his life. And the more he remembered his tantrum, the more he realized how unfair he had been. Maybe HE was the worst monster in the whole world.

But this time Arthur felt no urge to weep and wail. He had no time to feel ashamed or to wish he were as small as a flea on the knee of a flea.

With the speed of a Boeing 747, but in almost total silence, Arthur dismantled his barricades. He pushed his dresser back. He put his bookcase back together and put away all his clothes, his masks, his water pistols, and his creepy crawlies.

As best he could, he scraped off all the paint and ink from the window and hid the remains of his stuffed basset hound under his pillow. He glued the picture of his father back together.

Then he found a piece of chalk and, climbing up on his dresser, he drew three stems growing out of the trickles of pineapple juice, down to the middle of the wall. At the end of each stem he drew a daisy. Then in big letters he wrote below I LOVE MY DAD BEST OF ALL.

His heart thumping, Arthur finally opened the door. Behind it he discovered his dad, grinning from ear to ear, and holding a wonderful surprise in his arms.

Two big tears slid down Arthur's cheeks as he threw himself into his father's arms, right next to the surprise.

8
Not Aldo, not Banana

Arthur thought this must be the best Sunday of his whole life. He had just polished off two helpings of macaroni and cheese, a slice of butterscotch pie, and four and a half bananas.

Now he was sitting on his bed and stroking his brand-new baby basset hound.

As he petted it, he examined it all over. He admired its floppy ears, its long body, its droopy belly, its short legs, and its sad, sad eyes, the mark of a true basset hound.

Arthur knew that his basset

hound was much nicer than that low-slung purebred Quincy belonging to Annie McCubbin.

He hugged his puppy to his heart, and whispered in its ear, "Should I call you Aldo, after Al Doloroso, or should I call you Banana, after my favourite fruit?"

At the very instant he made up his mind, Arthur heard an ear-splitting *BADANG!* — and a voice yelling once again, "Arthur Goodberry, are you crazy or what? Didn't you see who I brought with me?"

Arthur knew Annie McCubbin was back with Quincy.

He hugged his little ball of fur tighter and went over to the window. He leaned out and looked at Ambidextrous Annie and said ᵘdly, "This is SUNDAY. He

has come straight from Africa.
My father rescued him single-
handed from a tribe of
orangutans!"

Arthur lifted Sunday high into the air. And, as Annie McCubbin looked on in amazement, he gave his puppy a big kiss — *SMACK* — right on the tip of its nose!